Rosa & Marco
and The Three Wishes

by Barbara Brenner
illustrated by Megan Halsey

BRADBURY PRESS • *New York*

Maxwell Macmillan Canada   *Toronto*
Maxwell Macmillan International
New York   Oxford   Singapore   Sydney

Bradbury Press
Macmillan Publishing Company
866 Third Avenue
New York, NY 10022

Maxwell Macmillan Canada, Inc.
1200 Eglinton Avenue East
Suite 200
Don Mills, Ontario M3C 3N1
Macmillan Publishing Company is part of
the Maxwell Communication Group of Companies.

First American edition
Printed and bound in Hong Kong by
South China Printing Company (1988) Ltd.
10 9 8 7 6 5 4 3 2 1

The text of this book is set in Gazette.
The illustrations are rendered in pen-and-ink and watercolor.
Typography by Julie Y. Quan

Library of Congress Cataloging-in-Publication Data
Brenner, Barbara.
Rosa and Marco and the three wishes / by Barbara Brenner ;
illustrated by Megan Halsey. —1st ed.
p.   cm.
Summary: Rosa and Marco receive three wishes from
a magical fish which they spend in comical fashion.
ISBN 0-02-712315-4
[1. Wishes—Fiction. 2. Brothers and sisters—Fiction.]
I. Halsey, Megan, ill. II. Title.
PZ7.B7518Ro   1992
[E]—dc20   90-26855

Rosa & Marco
and The Three Wishes

For Bill Hooks

—*B.B.*

To Marywood

—*M.H.*

Marco and his sister, Rosa,
were fishing.
They cast their net
and swished it around
in the waves.
Swish! Swish!

The morning passed.

The sun grew hot.

The waves lapped
at their feet.

Swish! Swish!

But no fish.

"I'm hungry," said Marco.

"I wish we could catch a fish."

Rosa was hungry, too.

It made her mad.

She said,"You are bad luck, Marco.

You keep the fish away."

Just then—

Swish, splash!

Something big was in the net!

The children pulled it in.

It was a great fish—
green as the sea,
with golden eyes.
"What luck!" said Rosa.
"We'll have fish for dinner."

The fish flapped in the net.

Flip! Flap!

"Poor fish!" said Marco.

The fish opened its mouth.

Marco said,

"This fish asks to be free."

"You are silly. Fish can't talk,"

said Rosa.

The fish opened its mouth again.

Marco said,

"This fish says if we let it go,

it will give us three wishes."

"What a baby you are," said Rosa.
"Fishes can't give wishes.
Give that fish to me."

Instead Marco gave the net a flip.

Flip! Flap!

The fish slipped into the waves.

With a swish of its tail,

it was gone.

Rosa was madder than before.

"Silly baby, now we have no dinner!"

"But we have three wishes,"
said Marco.

"Hush!" said Rosa.

"No more talk. No fishes and wishes!"

Marco said no more.

Soon he forgot

about the three wishes.

But he didn't forget
he was hungry.
He kept thinking about food.

Thinking about it, he said,
"How I wish I had a taco
with hot sauce."

Zoom! Zoom!

There in the air

was a taco with hot sauce!

"Rosa, look!" he cried.

"My wish came true!"

When his sister saw that
the wishes were real,
she was madder than ever.

"You are such a baby," she said.
"You could have wished for gold,
or a fine house,
or nice clothes.

"You wasted a wish on a taco."

Without thinking, Rosa said,

"I wish that taco

was on the end of your nose."

Zoom! Zoom!

The taco sailed through the air.

It landed smack on

Marco's nose.

It stuck there, sauce and all.

They pulled at it.

They twisted it.

Pull! Twist! Pull! Twist!

But the taco

would not come unstuck.

Rosa began to cry.

"What have I done?"

"You have made me a clown,"
cried Marco.

"And now we have
only one wish left."

Rosa looked at her poor little brother,
with a taco stuck on his nose.
Suddenly, she wasn't mad anymore.
She knew what she had to do.
"I wish that the taco
was off Marco's nose," she said.

Zoom! Zoom!

The taco was gone.

Marco sighed.

"Three wishes!

And things are no better."

"Well, at least
they're no worse," said Rosa.
"And we still have each other . . .
even if you are a baby."

She put her arm
around her brother.
And Rosa and Marco
went home.